A Note to Parents and Teachers

Kids can imagine, kids can laugh and kids can learn to read with this exciting new series of first readers. Each book in the Kids Can Read series has been especially written, illustrated and designed for beginning readers. Funny, easy-to-read stories, appealing characters, and engaging illustrations make for books that kids will want to read over and over again.

To make selecting a book easy for kids, parents and teachers, the Kids Can Read series offers three levels based on different reading abilities:

Level 1: Kids Can Start to Read

Short stories, simple sentences, easy vocabulary, lots of repetition and visual clues for kids just beginning to read.

Level 2: Kids Can Read with Help

Longer stories, varied sentences, increased vocabulary, some repetition and visual clues for kids who have some reading skills, but may need a little help.

Level 3: Kids Can Read Alone

Longer, more complex stories and sentences, more challenging vocabulary, language play, minimal repetition and visual clues for kids who are reading by themselves.

With the Kids Can Read series, kids can enter a new and exciting world of reading!

Pup and Hound
in Trouble

For Jayne and Tucker — S.H.

For Priscilla — L.H.

 Kids Can Read is a trademark of Kids Can Press Ltd.

Text © 2005 Susan Hood
Illustrations © 2005 Linda Hendry

Kids Can Press acknowledges the financial support of the Government of Ontario, through the Ontario Media Development Corporation's Ontario Book Initiative; the Ontario Arts Council; the Canada Council for the Arts; and the Government of Canada, through the BPIDP, for our publishing activity.

Published in Canada by
Kids Can Press Ltd.
29 Birch Avenue
Toronto, ON M4V 1E2

Published in the U.S. by
Kids Can Press Ltd.
2250 Military Road
Tonawanda, NY 14150

www.kidscanpress.com

The artwork in this book was rendered in pencil crayon on a sienna colored pastel paper.
The text is set in Bookman.

Series editor: Tara Walker
Edited by Yvette Ghione
Designed by Julia Naimska
Printed and bound in China

The hardcover edition of this book is smyth sewn casebound.
The paperback edition of this book is limp sewn with a drawn-on cover.

CM 05 0 9 8 7 6 5 4 3 2 1
CM PA 05 0 9 8 7 6 5 4 3 2 1

National Library of Canada Cataloguing in Publication Data

Hood, Susan
        Pup and hound in trouble / written by Susan Hood ; illustrated by Linda Hendry.

(Kids Can read)
ISBN 1-55337-676-5 (bound).   ISBN 1-55337-677-3 (pbk.)

1. Dogs — Juvenile fiction. I. Hendry, Linda II. Title. III. Series: Kids Can read (Toronto, Ont.)

PZ7.H758Pupi 2005   j813'.54   C2004-902614-3

Kids Can Press is a **corus™** Entertainment company

Pup and Hound
in Trouble

Written by Susan Hood

Illustrated by Linda Hendry

Kids Can Press

What was that?

What was that yelp?

4

Uh-oh! Oh, no!

Pup needs help!

Pup scooted from
his muddy bath.

Hound pulled him from

the horse's path!

Yuck! What a mess!

Time to clean up.

But when a frog jumped …

... so did Pup!

Pup swam and swam.

"Yip, yap! Yip, yelp!"

Uh-oh! Oh, no!

Pup needs help!

Pup was stuck

in weeds and muck.

"Quack! Quack! Quack!"

cried Mama Duck.

Hound paddled out

to rescue Pup.

He huffed and puffed

and pulled him up.

Pup shook and watered

all the flowers.

"YEOW!" said Cat,

who hated showers.

"Honk-honk! Honk-honk!"

"Yip, yap! Yip, yelp!"

Uh-oh! Oh, no!

Pup needs help!

Hound dashed in
and stood his ground.

But Pup was gone
when he turned around.

"Oink-oink! Neigh! MOOOO!"

Hound heard with alarm.

He turned and ran
to the old, red barn.

Hound found his friends
all looking up.
He held his breath
when he saw Pup.

Pup backed up,

spilling feed and grain.

It poured with a whoosh

like a warm spring rain.

A feast for all

was at their feet.

Hooray for Pup!

An afternoon treat!

What a good Pup!

Look what he'd done.

Everyone was glad ...

... except maybe one!